3/21

To all the inmates at the Moritz zoo,
from the world's luckiest zookeeper
—P.M.

KAR-BEN PUBLISHING®
An imprint of Lerner Publishing Group, Inc.
241 First Avenue North
Minneapolis, MN 55401 USA
www.karben.com

Image credits: Xinhua/Gil Cohen Magen/Getty Images, p. 32 (left); AHMAD GHARABLI/AFP/Getty Images, p. 32 (right).

Designed by Danielle Carnito
Main body text set in Aptifer Slab LT Pro. Typeface provided by Linotype AG.
The illustrations in this book were created with pencil, paper, Photoshop, and a pen tablet.

Library of Congress Cataloging-in-Publication Data

Names: Moritz, Pamela, 1965– author. | Weiser, Florence, illustrator.
Title: The great Passover escape / Pamela Moritz ; illustrated by Florence Weiser.
Description: Minneapolis, MN : Kar-Ben Publishing, Inc., a division of Lerner Publishing Group, Inc., [2021] | Audience: Ages 4–9. | Audience: Grades K–1. | Summary: "Chimp tries to talk his friends, Ellie and Kanga, out of escaping from the Biblical Zoo to find a seder, but ends up joining the escapade. How will they escape and where will they find a seder to attend?"— Provided by publisher.
Identifiers: LCCN 2020014638 (print) | LCCN 2020014639 (ebook) | ISBN 9781541588974 (library binding) | ISBN 9781541588981 (paperback) | ISBN 9781728417592 (ebook)
Subjects: CYAC: Passover—Fiction. | Seder—Fiction. | Zoo animals—Fiction. | Jerusalem Biblical Zoo—Fiction. | Israel—Fiction.
Classification: LCC PZ7.1.M6726 Gr 2021 (print) | LCC PZ7.1.M6726 (ebook) | DDC [E]—dc23

LC record available at https://lccn.loc.gov/2020014638
LC ebook record available at https://lccn.loc.gov/2020014639

Manufactured in the United States of America
1-47460-48025-5/15/2020

The Great Passover Escape

Pamela Moritz

illustrations by
Florence Weiser

KAR-BEN
PUBLISHING

It was evening at the Biblical Zoo in Jerusalem.

"The zoo will be closing for Passover tomorrow night,"
said Ellie the Elephant to her kangaroo friend, Kang.

"Closing? But *I* want to celebrate Passover," Kang said, peering over the wall. "I want to try that flat, crunchy thing people eat at the seder—it looks yummy."

"I think that's called a cracker," said Ellie, with a wise nod.

"No. I think it's a kind of toast," said Kang.

"It's matzah," said Chimp, their neighbor.
"Be quiet, both of you. I'm trying to sleep."

"Matzah?" said Ellie and Kang, looking at each other.

"Shhh!" said Chimp, closing her eyes.

Kang whispered to Ellie, "I have an idea. Let's sneak out of the zoo. Let's find a family and celebrate Passover with them. We can read from that book—what's it called?"

"A coloring book," said Ellie, nodding confidently.

"No, no," said Kang, scratching her nose. "It's a notebook."

"It's a haggadah," said Chimp with a sigh. "I'm trying to sleep. And you'll never be able to escape from the zoo. The walls are too high."

"How do you know?" asked Ellie.

"When I'm swinging from the trees, I can see over the walls," said Chimp.

"You'll see," said Ellie. "I'm sure we can do it."

"I don't think so,"
said Chimp.

The next evening, Kang took a deep breath, gave a huge jump, and jumped over the wall into Ellie's pen. He landed on her back.

"Are you sure I'm not too heavy?" he asked.

"You're perfect," said Ellie.

"You're noisy," harrumphed Chimp. She opened one eye just as Ellie opened the lock to the elephants' gate with her trunk.

"You don't know what you're doing," said Chimp.
"You'll get lost. Ellie will step on a car . . ."

"Oh, just come with us," said Kang.

Chimp shook her head.

"We could use your help," said Ellie.

"Humph," said Chimp. "Well, if you need my help, then I'll come with you."

And she scrambled across the trees and landed on Ellie's back.

"Zookeeper Shmulik cleans my habitat," Ellie said, lumbering toward the exit. "He told me all about Passover. He said that on Passover we say, 'Let all who are hungry come and eat' and I'm hungry!"

"Me too," said Kang. "Let's find a house with a family that celebrates Passover. Maybe we can join them before they start their wonderful Passover meeting."

"It's not a Passover meeting. It's a Passover party," said Ellie.

"A Passover seder," sighed Chimp.

"Shmulik told me that, in the Passover story, when Pharaoh wouldn't let the Jews leave Egypt, God sent Ten Planes so the Jews could leave," said Ellie.

"No. It was Ten Plates," corrected Kang.

"Ten Plagues," sighed Chimp.

"Yes," said Kang. "That's what I meant. And Shmulik said that finally God sent Morty to free the slaves."

"No, it was Milty," said Ellie with a nod.

"Moses," said Chimp.

"Yes, Moses, that's it."

The three friends arrived at the zoo's big entrance gate. It was locked.

"What should we do?" Kang asked Chimp. "It's too high for me to jump over."

Chimp quickly scrambled up the gate and over to the other side. Unlocking it, she swung the door open, and Ellie and Kang tiptoed out into the world.

"Hey—we did it! We're free!" exclaimed Kang.

"Just like in the Passover story!" said Ellie.

"I think the seder will be starting soon," said Ellie as they wandered into a little neighborhood. "Shmulik said there will be bitter and sweet foods to taste. Maybe they'll be lemon peels and mangoes! M-m-m!"

"No, they're—"

"Don't guess!" said Chimp, reaching up and gently closing Kang's mouth. "I'll tell you. The special foods are maror and haroset.

Maror is a bitter herb to remember how bitter the slaves' lives were. And haroset is the sweet food. It's made of nuts and apples. It's yummy, but it looks like the clay the slaves used to make bricks."

"Wow, Chimp," said Kang. "How do you know so much about Passover?"

"Well, I've lived in the Biblical Zoo since I was born," said Chimp. "Shmulik taught me all about Passover. It's my favorite holiday. I'm so excited to go to my first seder!"

"I'm glad you came with us," Ellie said as they came to a house with a beautifully set table.

"I see the special *circle* plate!" said Ellie.

"No, it's the *sample* plate," said Kang.

"*Seder* plate." Chimp shook her head as Ellie lumbered to the front door.

"I'm a little nervous knocking on a stranger's door," Ellie said to her friends.

Just then the door swung open, and it was ...

"Shmulik!" cried Ellie, Kang, and Chimp.

"Welcome!" Shmulik said to his friends.
"Let all who are hungry come and eat!"

About Passover

Passover is a weeklong holiday, celebrated in the spring, when we remember the exodus of the Jews from slavery in Egypt. Passover begins with a seder, a festive meal of prayers, readings, songs, and the tasting of symbolic foods.

About the Biblical Zoo

The Tisch Family Zoological Gardens in Jerusalem, also known as the Biblical Zoo, is an unusual 62-acre zoo containing more than 140 species of animals that are either mentioned in the Bible or are endangered species from around the world.

Rotem, a four-week-old female South African giraffe calf, stands near his mother at the Biblical Zoo.

A woman pushes a baby stroller past a family feeding a goat at Jerusalem's Biblical Zoo.